Hello Hippo!

Illustrated by Ian Newsham

DEAN

Hippo's New Shoes, Hippo's Birthday and
Goodnight Hippo first published 1989 by
The Parent and Child Programme,
an imprint of Reed International Books.
This edition published 1992 by Dean,
Michelin House, 81 Fulham Road, London SW3 6RB

© Reed International Books 1989

ISBN 0 603 55054 1

Produced by Mandarin
Printed in Hong Kong

Contents

To Parents

By sharing books together at home you can play a vital part in helping your child learn to read. These stories are designed to give the right support to your child in the early stages of reading – so that you can read together with confidence and enjoyment.

How to read this book together

▶ Make reading together a comfortable and special time.

▶ As the storyteller, you should read the words at the bottom of the page.

▶ After you have read your part, ask your child to join in with the words in the speech bubbles. All of these bubble words are repeated from words you have just read.

▶ Point to the words in the bubbles as they are read.

▶ On the first reading you could read the story and the first few bubbles yourself so your child thoroughly understands the idea before joining in.

Remember young children love repetition – and the more they read a story the more confident they will feel about joining in or reading their words alone.

Always use the pictures as they give lots of clues. Talk about what the characters are doing and encourage your child to predict what is going to happen next.

If your child is stuck just give the word yourself. This is far more helpful than sounding out individual letters.

Always praise good guesses – much of the skill in reading is in guessing or predicting what the word will be.

Always end reading together on a positive note by giving extra praise.

Hippo's New Shoes

by Jane Salt

Hippo's feet had grown so much
that he needed some new shoes.

So his mum and dad took him to
the shoe shop to buy some.

Hippo tried on some smart white
shoes with little holes in the front.

8

"They're too prickly," said Hippo.
"I don't like them."

Then Hippo tried on some slippers
with fierce green dragons.

"They're too scary," said Hippo.
"I don't like them."

So Hippo tried on some yellow
plastic shoes with sparkly bits.

"They're too bright," said Hippo.
"I don't like them."

Next Hippo tried on some trainers
with straps and go-faster stripes.

"Do you like them, Hippo?" they all asked.

"I love them," said Hippo. "They're just right."

16

Hippo's Birthday

by Jane Salt

One Monday Hippo and his
mum wrote some birthday-party
invitations together.

"Is it my birthday tomorrow?"
asked Hippo.
"No," said Mum, "not tomorrow."

On Tuesday Hippo saw his dad
hiding a parcel on the wardrobe.

"Is it my birthday tomorrow?" asked Hippo.

"No," said Dad, "not tomorrow."

On Wednesday Hippo's mum
bought sausages, cheese, little sticks
and biscuits with icing.

"Is it my birthday tomorrow?"
asked Hippo.
"No," said Mum, "not tomorrow."

On Thursday Hippo and his mum
made party hats with bright blue
paper and shiny stars.

"Is it my birthday tomorrow?"
asked Hippo.

"No," said Mum, "not tomorrow."

On Friday Hippo's dad made a big
yellow jelly in the shape of a fish.

"Is it my birthday tomorrow?"
asked Hippo.
"No," said Dad, "not tomorrow."

27

On Saturday Hippo saw a train
birthday cake in the shop. It had
four candles on the top.

"Is it my birthday tomorrow?"
asked Hippo.
"Yes," said Dad, "it's tomorrow."

On Sunday Hippo said, "It's my birthday today! Hurray!"

Hippo Learns
to Swim

by Diane Wilmer

"Let's go swimming," said Dad.

"What's swimming?" said Hippo.

"It's fun," said Dad. "You'll love it!"

"Here's the swimming pool," said Dad.

"It's very big!" said Hippo.

"Come on, Hippo, it's lovely," said Dad.

"No!" said Hippo. "It's wet!"

"Of course it's wet, it's water," said Dad.

"It's noisy water too!" said Hippo.

"Jump in, Hippo," said Dad.

"No!" said Hippo. "It's cold!"

"All hippos like water," said Dad.

"I don't like it," said Hippo.

"I'll teach you to swim," said Dad.

"Wait for me," said Hippo.

"One, two, three…jump!" said Dad.

"One, two, three…splash!" said Hippo.

"Clever Hippo!" said Dad.

"It's nice!" said Hippo.

"Swim to me, Hippo," said Dad.

"How do you swim?" said Hippo.

"Splash with your feet," said Dad.

"Splash! Splash! I can swim!"
said Hippo.

"We can swim together," said Dad.

"I'm a big hippo now," said Hippo.

"I love swimming," said Hippo.
"It's easy!"

Goodnight Hippo

by Jane Salt

It was past eight o'clock…

and Hippo had finished his bath.

"It's time for bed," said Dad.

But Hippo had a problem with
his pyjamas.

Dad made the pyjamas more comfortable.
"Now," he said, "it's time for bed."

But Hippo had to do his exercises.

Dad had some exercise too.
"Now," he said, "it's time for bed."

But Hippo had to write a letter.

Dad wrote a letter too.

"Now," he said, "it's time for bed."

But Hippo had to read a story.

Dad read a story too.

"Now," he said, "it's time for bed."

But Hippo had to find Teddy.

Dad found Teddy.

"Now," he said, "it's time for bed."

Hippo looked at Dad.

Dad looked at Hippo.
"Now!" said Dad firmly.

"Goodnight dressing-gown,"
said Hippo.

"Goodnight slippers," said Hippo.

"Goodnight rabbits," said Hippo.

"Goodnight ducks," said Hippo.

"Goodnight light," said Hippo.

"Goodnight Teddy," said Hippo.

"Goodnight Hippo," said Dad.

"Goodnight Dad," said Hippo and
he jumped into bed.

Dad tucked up Hippo and kissed
him goodnight.

"See you in the morning," said Dad.